To my Mommy and Daddy.
A special thank you to Marcy and Nejla S.

Text and Illustrations copyright © 2021 Jonah Seyum
Published by Tiny Global Footprints
To learn more, please visit: www.tinyglobalfootprints.com

Cover design and illustrations by Nejla Shojaie
Hardback ISBN-13: 978-1-7378577-0-9
Paperback ISBN-13: 978-1-7378577-1-6
eBook ISBN-13: 978-1-7378577-2-3

Library of Congress Control Number: 2021925056

Seyum, Jonah
What does Daddy do all day? / Jonah Seyum
ISBN-(hc) 13: 978-1-7378577-0-9

The alarm clock tells my dad to get ready for work. I get up and give my dad a big hug. "Can I go with you to work?" I ask.

But as always, he says, "Not today."
"Okay," I say with a sigh.

I love my dad; he's my hero.

He's been so nice to me since the minute I was born. Well, I don't remember the minute I was born, but I know he loves me a lot. My mom said he was so happy when I was born that he started crying, and he almost never cries.

My dad taught me how to play basketball,

how to whistle,

how to play with a PlayStation controller,

and how to cook delicious meals just like my
mom and grandma.

He also helps me with my schoolwork and plays with me when I'm done. I love spending time with him.

I often ask my dad to take time off from work to play with me, and most of the time he says, "No."

When he says no, I ask if I can go with him instead. But he says something like, "We can go on April thirty-first."

At first, I say, "Yay!" but then I say, "DAD!" because April 31st is not a real date.

What does he do at work?

Does he work with computers?

Does he do stuff with machines or robots?

What does it look like?

My mom works from home. She has meetings and calls almost all day.

Does my dad do the same at work? That's why I want to go with him so badly. I want to see where he works!

When Dad gets home from work, he's always very tired, but I want him to play with me. I have to drag him off the couch. If he'd let me go to work with him, I could help and he wouldn't come home so tired.

What do I have to do to get my dad to take me to work one day? I decide to do something really nice to make him happy. "Can I go to work with you now?" I ask him. The answer is still "No."

Sometimes he works overnight. I don't ask him to bring me then because I'm snoring. When he comes home around 7 a.m. I'm still snoring. He wakes me up at 8:15 to get to my class. Sometimes I am so tired that I fall asleep in the shower!

When my dad comes home from work I always hide. Hiding is one of my favorite things to do. I wait for my dad to find me.
Ooh, that gives me an idea.

I will hide in his car and sneak with him to work.

Somehow he sees me. "Son, back in the house you go," he says, laughing.
So close.

When my dad comes home from work, I always ask, "How was your day? What did you do at work?" I hope that getting him talking will get him to say yes to my next question: "Can I go with you tomorrow?" He shakes his head again.

I see Grandpa working in the garden. He says he's retired. Does Dad do the same work Grandpa used to do?

Does my dad tell people what to do? Does he sit at a desk? What does he do?!

If my dad would just bring me to his work, I could see everything and meet everyone. I don't know what to do to get him to take me to work.

In my imagination, he works somewhere cool with robots and big machines.

I've already tried begging him,

dressing like him,

and pretending it's April 31st.

I guess I'm going to have to do something sneaky.

I decide to follow him to work on my bike. Dad sees me and puts me back in the house. Man, he's hard to fool!

I give up. I'll have to live the rest of my life not knowing what Dad does at work all day. It's too bad for him, I would have been a good helper.

Out of nowhere, Dad says I can finally go to work with him tomorrow! I am so excited that I wake up at 6 a.m. and get ready before my dad.

As he drives me to work with him, I sing, "My daddy is taking me to work today, la la la la la."

We arrive at his workplace. Finally, my dream of seeing what he does is coming true.

As we walk to the front door, my dad slows down. There's a sign on the door.

Then my shoulders drop, and I sigh sadly.

Sorry, we are closed today due to the thunderstorm's electric outage

The next day, my dad asks me if I want to go play soccer. I'm sure he's just trying to cheer me up, but I say, "Okay," and get ready to go.

This doesn't look like a soccer field. It's a surprise! He brought me to his work! I jump up and down with excitement. I finally get to see what my dad does!

I guess my prediction was right. My dad does work with computers and cool machines.

I can't wait to grow up and be just like him.

I want to inspire kids like me to write books just like I did.

Thank you for reading my awesome book.

ABOUT THE AUTHOR

Jonah Seyum is eight years old and in 3rd grade. He loves hanging out with his family, especially his parents and his 22 cousins who live in Minneapolis, Atlanta, Orlando, and Denver. He also enjoys playdates with his school friends. He loves playing soccer and basketball and reading the Diary of a Wimpy Kid series. His favorites foods are steak, burgers, rice, and beans. Jonah has been to eleven countries and enjoys learning new languages and dancing to Eritrean music.

Tiny Global Footprints

For more information, visit our site:
www.tinyglobalfootprints.com

Get our first book:
The Search for Elephants in Thailand

Get our second book:
Finding My Amigo in Cuba

Get our third book:
Basketball or soccer?

Made in the USA
Middletown, DE
16 October 2022